There's So Much More to Wear Than Hair

Written & Illustrated by Sarah Kravchuk

I woke up one morning to find
On my pillow, a pile of my hair.
Not one or two or three strands
But almost all were resting there.

"Everyone will notice me,"
I cried without a care, but wait...
There's so much more to wear than hair.

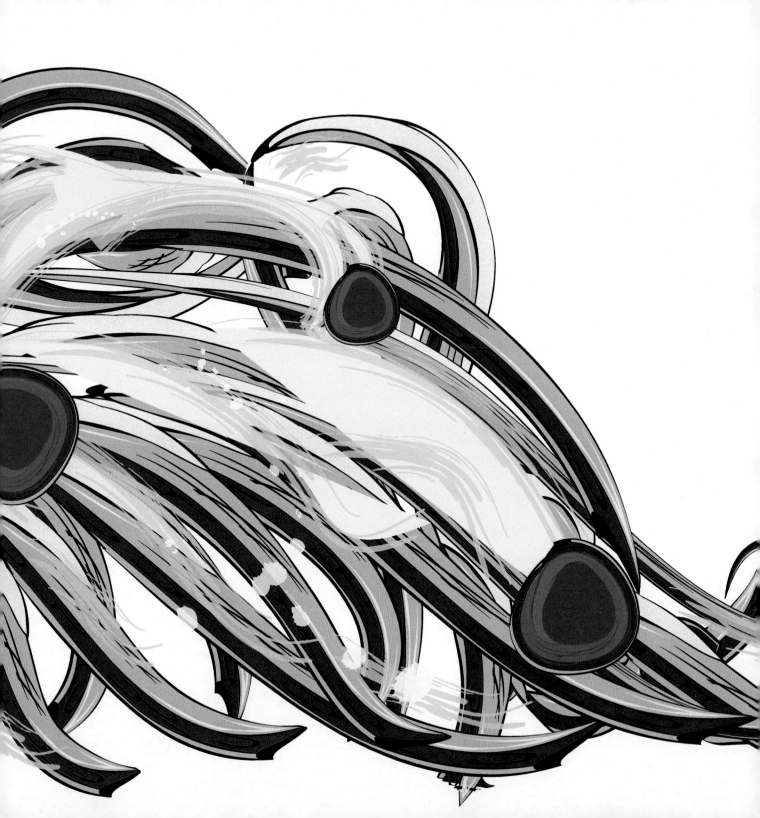

Like a big bowl of spaghetti,
With sauce and lots of cheese,
Braided into pigtails with
Meatball bows, if you please.

Or maybe a flower garden
Of red, blue and green,
Daisies, tulips and roses,
Are sure to make a scene.

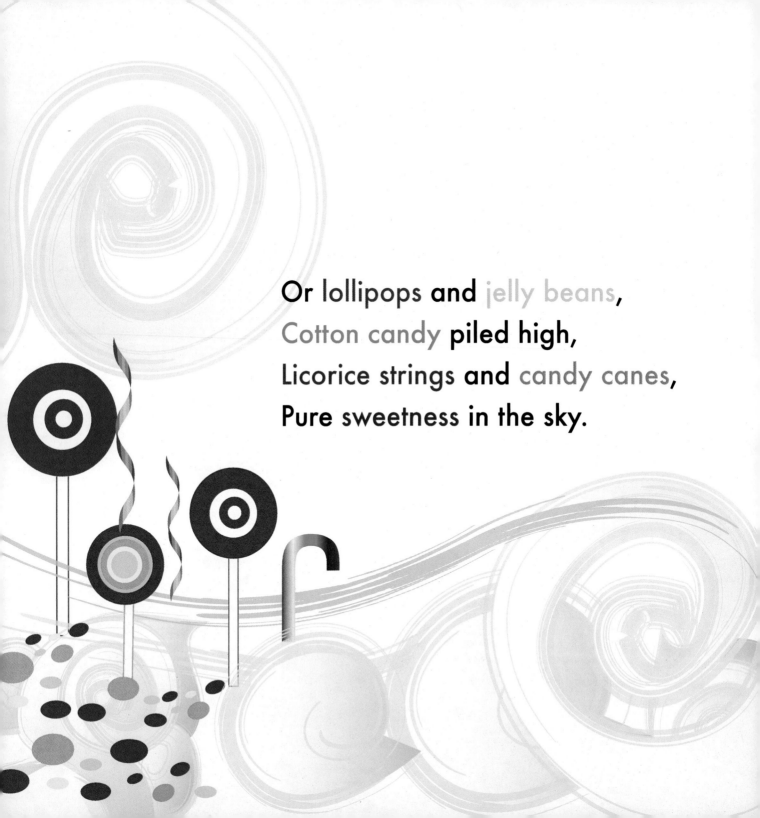

Or lollipops and jelly beans,
Cotton candy piled high,
Licorice strings and candy canes,
Pure sweetness in the sky.

There's so much more to wear
than hair.
Be creative, get excited,
Try these others if you dare...

Building blocks and wooden logs,
Stacked in every direction
Tiny toys, linked together
Into a tower of perfection.

Paintbrushes **and** crayons,
Markers **and** glitter **too,**
Construction paper **shapes**
Stuck together with lots of glue.

A wig made out of silly straws,
Plastic forks and   ,
Atop, a tin foil spaceship,
To fly me to the moon.

There's so much more to wear than hair...

Like, the finest scarves I've ever seen, baseball caps,

pirate hats, **or a crown** fit for a queen.

Weeks and months of treatment
And lots of medical care,
Words like chemo and radiation,
Floating around me in the air.

Cancer Radiation Hospital Treatments Me

Sickness Hairloss tired weak

ion
Radiation
CHEMOTHERAPY
MEDICATION
treatment
surgery
doctors
pills
AHH!!

I may get weak and tired,
And nap with baby bear
But when I awake, I'll discover
Something new, growing up there...

PING! PING! PING!
I heard atop my little head.
Not a plant, or green grass but
My first new hair instead.

"HURRAY," I shouted,
Looking in the mirror to see,
Lots of little hairs
Have returned, just to me!

The End

Made in the USA
Monee, IL
24 December 2021

87084349R00019